Welcome to Innerstar University! At this imaginary, one-of-a-kind school, you can live with your friends in a dorm called Brightstar House and find lots of fun ways to let your true talents shine. Your friends at Innerstar U will help you find your way through some challenging situations, too.

When you reach a page in this book that asks you to make a decision, choose carefully. The decisions you make will lead to more than 20 different endings! (*Hint:* Use a pencil to check off your choices. That way, you'll never read the same story twice.)

Want to try another ending? Read the book again—and then again. Find out what would have happened if you'd made *different* choices. Then head to www.innerstarU.com for even more book endings, games, and fun with friends.

Innerstar Guides

Every girl needs a few good friends to help her find her way. These are the friends who are always there for **you.**

Emmy

A brave girl who loves swimming and boating

Isabel

A confident girl with a funky sense of style

Riley

A good sport, on the field and off

Paige

A nature lover who leads hikes and campus cleanups

Amber

An animal lover and
a loyal friend

Neely

A creative girl who loves
dance, music, and art

Logan

A super-smart girl
who is curious about
EVERYTHING

Shelby

A kind girl who is there
for her friends—and loves
making NEW friends!

Innerstar U Campus

1. Rising Star Stables
2. Star Student Center
3. Brightstar House
4. Starlight Library
5. Sparkle Studios
6. Blue Sky Nature Center

7. Real Spirit Center

8. Five-Points Plaza

9. Starfire Lake & Boathouse

10. U-Shine Hall

11. Good Sports Center

12. Shopping Square

13. The Market

14. Morningstar Meadow

[Y] ou check your watch as you run through the front doors of the Star Student Center. 12:47. You have only a few minutes to grab lunch before the cafeteria closes.

Something catches your eye on the bulletin board just inside the doors. It's a gold flyer announcing the Innerstar University film festival—a marathon movie-watching event where you can see some of the best student-made movies. There's a contest to enter, with a deadline in two weeks.

You haven't given the contest much thought. You've never made your own movies before, other than a few short, silly videos you shot of your friends using your camera. Besides, you have other things on your mind right now: like whether you can still get a slice of pizza from today's lunch special.

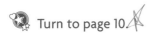 Turn to page 10.

You're in luck! There's one shriveled-looking slice of pizza left, which you grab just before the cafeteria lady takes the tray away. Then you search the lunchroom to see if any of your friends are still there. Logan waves from a corner, where she's sitting with Riley and Neely.

As you slide into a seat across from your friends, you realize they're talking about the movie contest.

"I'm recording my own version of *Cinderella*," says Neely excitedly. "Actually, I'm directing it—but I think I can do both." There's a hint of worry in her freckled face, but you know Neely will make a great film. She's one of the most creative girls you know.

Logan wants to do a short documentary on bean plants. "My camera has a time-lapse mode that'll take a picture of the plant every hour. Then I can play back the shots in fast motion," she says, "to make it look as if the plant is growing right before your eyes!" Her own green eyes glaze over, as if she's already watching the movie in her mind.

"How about you, Riley?" you ask between bites of pizza.

"Hmm . . . ," says Riley, twirling a strand of blonde hair around her finger. "I'm thinking about doing a video of 'Innerstar U's winning moments'—you know, like going through some of the soccer games we've recorded and pulling out the best goals and passes."

You nod, thinking, *Wow, another great idea.*

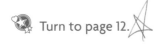 Turn to page 12.

"What are you going to do?" Neely asks you.

You take a sip of your drink before answering. "I'm not sure," you say. "I guess I'm not much of a moviemaker."

Neely shrugs good-naturedly. "That's okay," she says. "You could always help one of us if you wanted to."

"Yes!" adds Logan. "That would be fun."

Riley nods her head, too. "I could definitely use help sorting through old soccer videos," she says.

You glance around the table at your friends, who are all being sweet about this. You're game for helping out on a movie—it sounds like a great way to learn more about moviemaking. But which project do you want to work on most?

If you help Neely with *Cinderella*, turn to page 20.

If you help Logan with her bean-plant documentary, turn to page 14.

If you help Riley with "Innerstar U's Winning Moments," turn to page 17.

You tell Neely that you think you'll make a better actor than camera girl. You're hoping for a great part, like Cinderella or the fairy godmother, but those parts have already been cast.

Neely tells you that Cinderella will be played by Devin, which surprises you. Instead of the kind, blonde-haired Cinderella you grew up reading about, the star of this movie will be a stubborn redhead. You've crossed paths with Devin before, and you know she can be super-competitive—and sometimes downright mean.

Neely sees the look on your face and reads you like a book. "Oh, I know," she says. "Devin can be tough, but she's a really good actress. Just give her a chance."

Then Neely runs down the other characters, counting them off on her fingers: "Isabel is the fairy godmother, Megan is the evil stepmother, Kayla is one of the stepsisters, and"—Neely points at you—"I'm hoping that *you* will be the other stepsister."

Playing an ugly stepsister isn't exactly your dream role, but you know that you'll have fun acting out scenes with your friends Kayla and Megan. And when Neely tells you that Prince Charming will be played by a puppy, you're sold. *That alone will be worth the price of admission,* you think.

 Turn to page 34.

Logan is thrilled that you want to help her with her bean-plant documentary. She wants to start right away, so after lunch, you follow her to the Blue Sky Nature Center to find a bean to plant.

"I hope Paige is there," says Logan, hurrying along the path.

You nod in agreement, trying to catch your breath. Your friend Paige volunteers at the nature center and has a super-green thumb. When you spot her blonde head just inside the greenhouse, you breathe a sigh of relief. This project is off to a great start!

Paige shows you where she has a bunch of potted bean plants at different stages of growth. Some are small green shoots just popping out of the soil, and others are nearly a foot tall. She brings you and Logan a small clay pot and potting soil, along with a bean to plant. Tiny roots have sprouted from the end. "It's a broad bean," Paige explains.

Logan sucks in her breath. "You mean like a fava bean?" she asks. "Cool! This is one of the earliest vegetables ever planted. I read somewhere that scientists found the remains of these plants from as far back as 6500 B.C.!"

6500 B.C.? Logan is full of facts like that. You stare at the bean and give it a little nudge with your finger. Huh. Looks like a regular old bean to you.

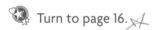 Turn to page 16.

Paige fills the pot with soil and uses her finger to make a hole. "Drop in the bean," she says to Logan.

Logan sets the bean into the hole as carefully as if it were a gemstone. Then Paige covers the bean with dirt and gives it a healthy drink with a watering can. "Water it every day," she says, "and keep it in a sunny window."

Logan frowns. "I don't think we get enough sunlight in our rooms at Brightstar House," she says. "Could we keep the plant here in the greenhouse?"

Paige hesitates and then nods toward a corner, where a few young plants are soaking up the sun. "That's a safe, sunny place," she says, "but I don't know where you'll set up your camera."

Logan explores the greenhouse wall, looking for a ledge where she can set the camera. "I think we need a tripod," she decides. "I'll run to the yearbook office and see if I can borrow one from Shelby."

 Turn to page 18.

You love Riley's energy and enthusiasm. Any project you do with her is sure to be fun. "Sign me up, coach," you say when she finishes describing her movie project.

"Great!" she says. "Can't wait to work with you."

That's just a few hours before Riley calls to say that she suddenly came down with the stomach flu. You grab your own stomach for a second, hoping it wasn't the cafeteria pizza. So far, so good.

"I'm sorry," you say to Riley. "Does that mean the movie's off?"

"No," says Riley. "Becca is helping me out, too. Maybe you guys can work together. She might be down at the yearbook office right now finding video clips."

You know Becca a little bit from soccer. She's involved in lots of sports on campus, actually, so maybe she'll be a good partner for this movie. You head down to the yearbook office at the student center to see if she's still there.

 Turn to page 19.

While Logan's gone, you rearrange some of the plants on the shelf to make sure your bean plant gets some good light. You're rotating the pot when Jamie, a classmate of yours, steps up beside you.

"Is this the famous bean-plant project?" she asks, flipping her brown hair over one shoulder as she leans in to get a better look.

You nod, but you say nothing. Jamie is one of your least favorite people at Innerstar U, and you'd rather not get into a conversation with her. Whenever you do, you usually end up regretting it.

"Logan was telling me about the project," Jamie says. "She said I might be able to help. What do you say?"

What you *want* to say is "no way." Jamie is acting nice right now, but working with her on team projects can be, well, *complicated*. What was Logan thinking?

 If you let Jamie be a part of the project, turn to page 23.

 If you tell her that you and Logan have it covered, turn to page 24.

Sure enough, you spot dark-haired Becca sitting in the yearbook office in front of a computer, watching a video of a soccer game.

"Becca," you say, tapping her on the shoulder. "Riley sent me here to help you out. Is there anything I can do?"

"Sure," says Becca, handing you a stack of DVDs. "You can start watching some of these on the computer over there. We have a ton to get through."

You look at the date on the first disk. This one's old— from before you joined the soccer team. You watch the game slowly, waiting for the first "winning moment."

From behind you, you hear Becca giggling. "Hey, watch this," she says, replaying part of the video on her screen. It's a scene from a rainy soccer match, and you see a muddy player going for the ball and then sliding into a horrific wipeout. You burst out laughing, too.

"Guess who that is," says Becca.

You squint at the screen. "Is that . . . you?" you ask.

"Yup," says Becca, "that's me. Do you think we should add it to the 'winning moments'?"

 Turn to page 28.

Who can say no to *Cinderella*? Especially when Neely pulls her sketchbook out of her backpack and shows you some of the costumes she's been thinking about.

"Isabel is going to help me make some of these out of old costumes at U-Shine Hall," Neely tells you.

Okay, now you're sold. Isabel is a friend of yours who is always putting together fun new outfits, like the beautiful fairy costumes she helped you create for the spring dance recital. With Neely behind the camera and Isabel's fashion-design skills, this'll be an amazing movie, and you can't wait to be a part of it.

"So, do you want to help me film the play? I could use a second camera girl," says Neely.

Before you can answer, she says, "Or, wait! I also need another actor in the play. Someone just dropped out."

 If you help out as Camera Girl Number 2,
turn to page 22

 If you want to play a role onstage, turn to page 13

Before rehearsal, you stop at the student center's year-book office to check out a camcorder. Your friend Shelby is there, and she gives you a quick tutorial of how to use the camera. Then you slide the strap around your wrist and head to U-Shine Hall.

When you get to the main auditorium, you see Neely and the cast of *Cinderella* onstage.

"Hey!" says Neely, waving to you as she steps down off the stage. "We're still rehearsing this scene, but you can take some footage, just for practice."

Sounds good, you think. You're not sure about this film-ing thing. You're a little nervous about messing up.

Neely helps you set up your camera on a tripod off-stage. You record the next hour of rehearsal, playing with different camera angles and zooming in and out to capture the expressions on the actors' faces.

Through the viewfinder, you notice that Kayla, one of the actors playing an evil stepsister, looks really nervous. *I probably would be, too,* you think to yourself, which makes you feel better about your decision to be on *this* side of the camera instead of onstage.

 Turn to page 25.

You don't want to work with Jamie, but you don't feel right about excluding her, either. After all, when *you* didn't have a movie project to work on, lots of people invited you to join them. Maybe it's time to pass on that invitation to someone else.

"Sure, you can help out," you say reluctantly.

Jamie looks a little surprised—and grateful—that you said yes, which makes you feel like you did the right thing.

When Logan returns with the tripod, the three of you set up a schedule for when to water the plant. There's not a lot to do except give it a drink now and then and watch it grow.

 Turn to page 26.

"I don't know, Jamie," you say, without looking up. "It's a pretty simple project. I don't think we need more people working on it."

Jamie is silent for a moment—which is unusual. Then she says sharply, "Suit yourself. Sounds boring, anyway."

You're relieved when Jamie leaves. Logan shows up a few minutes later with a tripod, and she sets up her camera in front of the potted bean. Then you and Logan work out a watering schedule: she'll water the bean each morning, and you'll check on it in the evening to see if the soil is still moist.

On your way out of the greenhouse, you see that the nature center is open till eight o'clock. That'll give you plenty of time to check the plant after dinner each night.

Turn to page 27.

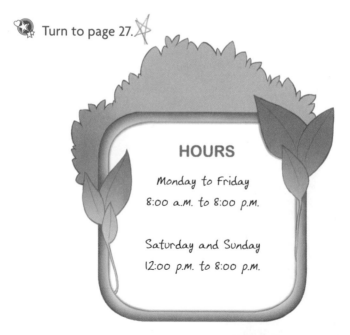

HOURS

Monday to Friday
8:00 a.m. to 8:00 p.m.

Saturday and Sunday
12:00 p.m. to 8:00 p.m.

After rehearsal, you head back to your room at Brightstar House and replay the footage. At first, you're pretty focused on your videography skills—or *lack* of skills. You zoomed in so far on Kayla's face that you can see every freckle. But you completely cut off Cinderella, played by a redheaded actor named Devin. And when Devin walked across the stage, you lost track of her and got a close-up shot of the stage curtains instead.

When you finally stop picking out your every mistake, you notice some serious drama playing out onstage.

Kayla and Devin are running through the same scene over and over again, and Kayla keeps messing up her lines. Devin is whispering something to her. At first you think Devin is reminding her of what to say, but when you turn up the volume, you realize that Devin is poking fun at Kayla for messing up.

"Have you lost your *memory*?" she asks snidely. "Did the fairy godmother cast a spell on you?"

Kayla says nothing, but you can see the slow burn of embarrassment creeping up her face.

In between scenes, you notice a lot of other Devin-drama moments. She gets into an argument with Isabel about costumes, and she and Megan—who plays the evil stepmother—have it out backstage, too. You wonder what's up with Devin. *Is she just having an off day?*

🌟 Turn to page 48.

Jamie is good about taking her share of watering shifts, but when you run into her at the greenhouse three days later, she seems bored.

"The plant's growing," she says, pointing toward the little green shoot popping out of the dirt, "but this project is about as exciting as watching paint dry. I think I might help Amber with her pet movie instead."

At first, Jamie's words sting. But you heard about your friend Amber's project over breakfast this morning, and you have to admit, it *does* sound like fun.

Animal-loving Amber is recording puppies and kittens at Pet-Palooza, the pet day-care center where she volunteers. Your friend Shelby is showing her how to dub voices over the top so that it looks as if the pets are talking. If you had it to do all over again, *you* probably would have chosen that movie project, too.

You glance at the bean plant, which is showing no signs of doing anything spectacular over the next few days. Logan can probably handle things from here on out. Should you ask Amber if you can help with her project instead?

 If you decide to switch projects, turn to page 56.

If you stick with the bean-plant project, turn to page 30.

You check on the bean after dinner that night, which you know is kind of silly, because Paige watered it just a few short hours ago. But Neely wants to see the plant, so you decide to visit your bean and to take Neely with you.

As you're showing Neely the potted bean, she shares with you some advice that her grandma gave to her about taking care of plants. "Some people talk to plants," says Neely, "but my grandma sings to them."

Neely leans in toward the pot and hums a few notes. When she hears you giggling (you can't help it!), she straightens back up. "What?" she asks, laughing along with you. "I'm just saying—it can't hurt."

You smile and shake your head. You're not sure if you'll ever sing to the bean plant. But as the sun sinks in the sky and the light in the greenhouse grows dimmer, you can't help talking to the plant. "Good night, little bean," you say, giving the pot a gentle pat.

 Turn to page 42.

Becca's wipeout scene gets you both thinking about how funny it would be to add a few wipeouts to the movie. You don't have any trouble finding them. It seems as if there are more silly soccer moments than there are spectacular ones!

You start saving the clips, and after an hour or so of searching—and giggling—you and Becca compare the clips you've gathered.

You know most of the girls in the clips. There's Neely, gearing up for a kick—and missing the ball entirely. There's Amber, getting tangled up in another player's legs.

The best clip, though, is of curly-haired Shelby scoring a goal—for the wrong team. You and Becca have to watch that one three times because it's so funny.

"What are you guys laughing about?" someone asks from behind you. It's *Shelby*.

 Turn to page 31.

You squat down to get a good look at the bean plant. It looks like a tiny green person, bent over and struggling to stand up. It's actually pretty cute! You know Logan will be thrilled to see it tomorrow morning.

Logan. She's so excited about this project. You decide that you can't abandon her midway through, no matter how fun Amber's project sounds. You tell Jamie to go ahead, that you and Logan have this project covered. And you carry on with your watering schedule, watching the little plant grow a bit more every day.

After a week and a half, Logan turns off the camera. She downloads the shots onto her computer and strings them together into a movie. When she plays it for you, it's really cool, but it's awfully short. It's amazing how ten days can be compressed into about ten seconds on-screen.

"I guess I thought it would last longer," says Logan with a sigh. "Maybe we should slow it down." She tries that, and you watch the movie again. This time, it takes about sixty seconds, and the plant grows much more slowly.

"It just seems like it's missing something," says Logan, slumping back in her chair.

You have to admit it—she's right. Amber's animal project is sounding better and better. Jamie told you over lunch today that Amber even has a scene where a *dog* is dancing to music!

 Turn to page 32.

"Um, nothing," says Becca before you can speak. "We found some good footage for our 'Winning Moments' movie."

"Oh, let me see!" says Shelby, stepping closer.

Becca puts up her hands to cover the screen. "No, not yet!" she says. "You'll have to wait till the movie premieres, just like everybody else."

"Alright, alright," Shelby says. "At least I know there won't be any video of me in there. I didn't have too many 'winning moments' on the soccer field last season," she jokes good-naturedly.

It's true—Shelby had a pretty rough season. You wonder how she'll feel about you featuring the clip of her not-so-winning goal in your movie. Will she think it's as funny as you and Becca do?

If you say something to Becca later about pulling the clip, turn to page 37.

If you stay quiet, hoping that Shelby will be okay with it, turn to page 33.

Dancing dogs. Amber's movie is going to be pretty hard to compete with. But as Logan plays the bean-plant movie again, it suddenly occurs to you that the growing *plant* looks as if it's dancing, too.

"Hey, Logan," you say, pressing the pause button on her keyboard. "We should add music!"

You search the "purchased" playlist on Logan's computer and click on an upbeat song by your favorite band, the Strawberries.

"But that song is over three minutes, and the movie is only *one* minute," says Logan.

"Maybe we can make it longer," you reassure her, "with a little editing magic."

That's when the fun begins. You and Logan figure out how to play the movie forward *and* backward. You play certain parts over and over again because you like the way they look. By the time the movie is done, you and Logan are giggling like crazy. It's so much fun!

 Turn to page 36.

You convince yourself that Shelby won't mind a clip or two featuring her soccer slipups. After all, the first one Becca showed you was of herself, muddy and unhappy. If Becca can laugh at herself, Shelby can, too, right?

The more you think about the movie, the funnier you're sure it will be. In fact, you start thinking about all the *other* goof-ups there must be on video in the yearbook office. Maybe you can find some funny dive-team moments, or cheerleading slipups, or even capsized canoe clips from down at the lake. The kite-flying contest must have some tangled-up moments, too. The possibilities are endless!

Capturing "Innerstar U's Funniest Campus Clips" will take time, though. You don't know how you can do that and work on the soccer video, too.

Luckily, Riley is feeling better the next day. When she pokes her head into your room, you tell her that you've come up with an idea for a movie of your own.

"That's okay," says Riley. "Becca and I can pull our movie together—now that I'm feeling better."

"Are you sure?" you ask Riley. She still looks a little pale.

"Definitely," says Riley. "I'm on my way to the yearbook office right now. Want to come?"

 Turn to page 38.

Neely gets you a script, which you study during some downtime in class that afternoon. Later, when it's time for rehearsal, you wind your way through U-Shine Hall until you reach the main auditorium.

You must be early, because Kayla is the only actor onstage. She blows her brown bangs off her forehead and gives you a smile of relief. "Boy, am I glad you're here," she whispers as you step onstage beside her. "Megan and Devin are really going at it."

"What do you mean?" you ask.

"Shh," she says, raising a finger to her lips. "Look . . ." Kayla tiptoes toward the backstage area and points around the heavy curtains.

You hear Megan's voice before you can actually see her. "But you're being such a drama queen," she says to Devin, who is standing next to her in the shadowy backstage area. "We need to work together."

"You're just mad because you didn't get the part of Cinderella," Devin spouts back, her finger in Megan's face. "But you're the *perfect* evil stepmother. Neely made the right call." You jump back behind the curtain as Devin comes storming toward you. She brushes past you without a hello.

Megan is close behind her, but she stops when she sees you and Kayla. "Oh, hey," she says. "Sorry about that. 'Devin-ella' is driving me crazy. I don't know if I can stand her much longer."

 Turn to page 40

When you get the e-mail telling you that your movie was accepted into the film festival, you and Logan do a happy dance of your own. You go to the festival together and hold your breath, waiting for your movie to pop up on-screen. You hope the audience likes it just as much as you do.

There it is! Your bean plant springs from the potting soil like a little green inchworm. It stands up slowly and flaps its leaves, like arms, to the beat of the music. It sways to the left and sways to the right. It shrinks and grows, shrinks and grows, until the music is almost over, and then the plant takes a slow little bow back toward the earth—the perfect finish.

The audience bursts into appreciative laughter. *Yes!*

 Turn to page 39.

As you and Becca leave the yearbook office, she's chatting excitedly about the new take on your movie. "People are going to love it—especially the soccer players," she says. "I can't wait to see their faces when they see their 'embarrassing moments' on-screen!"

You flash on Shelby's face, remembering the way it looked in the video right after she scored a goal for the wrong team. "I'm not sure they *will* love it," you say. "Some of them will think it's funny, but some of them might not. I don't want to hurt or embarrass anybody."

Becca looks crushed. "But I thought you liked this idea," she says, whining a little.

"I did," you admit. "But that was before I thought it through. Becca, I really don't think it's a good idea. Let's just focus on the *real* winning moments, okay?"

Becca doesn't say anything. She stares at you, tight-lipped, and then shrugs and walks away toward the bakery.

You sigh. This project is going to be tough, especially if Riley doesn't bounce back from the flu pretty soon.

 Turn to page 52.

Two hours later, you're still searching videos in the year-book office. Riley is just leaving as Shelby walks in.

"Hey," Shelby says to you. "What are you working on?"

When you tell Shelby about your plan to feature the funniest campus clips in your video, she smiles, but she doesn't seem to think it's as funny as you do. There's a hint of worry in her hazel eyes.

"I bet you'll find lots of great stuff," Shelby says. "But you should probably get permission from everybody in your video. That's what I do when I'm putting photos in the yearbook."

Permission? That sounds like a lot of work, especially given how many clips you're planning to use. You would practically have to ask every girl on campus, and then your movie wouldn't be the funny surprise you're envisioning.

Shelby is staring at you with her "trust me on this" expression. What do you do?

 If you take Shelby's advice and get permission, turn to page 43.

 If you decide you're okay without it, turn to page 51.

After your movie ends, even Jamie taps you on the shoulder to congratulate you. "Looks like you found a way to make the project less boring," she says. You know that's about as good a compliment as you're going to get from her, so you say thanks.

Amber's movie is up next, and it's fun, too. It ends with a scene showing a puppy and kitten cuddling. A caption pops up that says, "A loyal friend stays by your side."

Logan whispers in your ear, "Sounds like you. Thanks for sticking with me, friend."

You grin at Logan. You're glad now that you stuck with the project, and proud that you found a way to make it more fun—*together*.

The End

It doesn't take long before you see exactly what Megan is talking about. "Devin-ella" gets impatient when Kayla can't remember her lines, which makes Kayla stumble over them all the more.

Then Devin argues with Isabel about the gown she chose for Cinderella to wear to the ball. Devin sees Isabel's fairy godmother outfit and thinks she should wear that one instead.

"But see? It has wings," Isabel explains, much more patiently than you would have. "Cinderella doesn't wear fairy wings."

"Maybe we could just cut them off," Devin says, a suggestion that horrifies Isabel.

Neely tries to smooth things over by giving everyone a fifteen-minute break. She looks pretty stressed. Directing and filming a show like this in a couple of weeks is a big job, and Devin isn't making it any easier.

You wish you could help Neely more, but when you catch sight of Devin and Isabel squabbling backstage, your head starts to hurt. *Not even the fairy godmother's magic wand could save this production,* you think to yourself. *What did I get myself into?*

 Turn to page 58.

The next day after morning classes, you're walking through Five-Points Plaza. You see Logan heading your way from the nature center. "There you are!" she says. "I was hoping to run into you. Have you checked on our bean today?"

"No!" you say. "I thought you were doing the morning shift."

"I *am*," says Logan, "but you have to see this." She grabs your hand and pulls you along toward the greenhouse. When you get inside and walk toward your potted bean, you can't believe your eyes. There's a little green stalk sprouting from the soil, one leaf bowed down like a tiny head and two leaf "arms" unfolding out to the sides. You're shocked.

"I know!" says Logan. "I've never seen a bean plant grow so quickly before. Usually it takes a couple of days to get to this point."

The little plant looks so green and healthy. You make a silent vow to keep it that way.

You visit the plant again that night and give it a good drink of water, and then—when no one's looking—you lean down and hum a lullaby. Who knows? Maybe Neely's grandma was right!

 Turn to page 44.

Shelby has been on the yearbook staff for a long time. You respect her opinion—she'd never steer you wrong.

Shelby helps you create a permission form, and as you work your way through the videos, choosing funny clips, you start e-mailing the permission form to your friends and other students featured in the clips.

Most of the girls sign the form right away because they're excited to be part of the movie. Some of them ask to see the clips first, but that's okay. You probably would, too, if someone said you had a surprise role in an upcoming campus comedy!

One of the girls you approach for permission is Becca. You have this great clip of her walking along the edge of the fountain in Five-Points Plaza. You're not sure who shot the video, but the filmmaker sure does squeal when Becca slips and falls into the water. The next five seconds—when Becca jumps back out, shocked and soaking wet—are pretty priceless.

Becca e-mails back to say that you can use the clip. "I don't need to see it first," she writes. "I remember the moment all too well!"

 Turn to page 45.

The next morning, Logan finds you right away at breakfast. She's so excited, she can hardly speak. "You *have* to see our plant," she says. "It's incredible!"

And it is. The plant has several more leaves now and is much taller! Logan is convinced that you've discovered a magic bean—or a magic method for growing beans. "But what are we doing that's so special?" she asks. "We're giving it good sun and water, but Paige does that with all her plants. What's different here?"

You flash back to the lullaby you sang to the plant last night. Could that be what's making the plant grow? You want to help Logan find answers, but you're afraid that if you mention the singing, she might laugh at you.

If you tell Logan about Neely's grandma's advice, turn to page 68.

If you shrug and say nothing, turn to page 46.

Then Becca e-mails again and says that maybe she should ask for *your* permission, too. She has a great clip of you messing up on the soccer field. "Would you like to see it," she writes, "to make sure it's something you're okay with my showing?"

You appreciate that Becca asked. When she describes the clip—a moment when you wound up to kick the ball and ended up landing on your back—you laugh and tell her to go ahead and use it. "Now we're even," you joke.

 Turn to page 47.

You continue doing what you're doing, and the plant keeps growing—a few inches every day, which seems incredible. After a week, Logan has an amazing video of the growth. She shows it to you, and you're blown away. You two will win this contest for sure!

A week later, you learn that you *did* win a place in the film festival. You gather in the theater at U-Shine Hall with your friends surrounding you.

As the screen lights up, you catch sight of Jamie in the row in front of you. You feel a little guilty for excluding her from this project, especially after seeing how well it turned out. You hope she's not still mad, but you can't worry about that now—your magic bean movie is about to start.

The video is short, but it's a hit. As the bean plant sprouts from the potted dirt and stands up to do its little growth dance, its leaves waving from side to side, you hear your friends oohing and ahhing around you.

 Turn to page 50.

When you finally pull all your clips together into a ten-minute movie, you're pretty happy with it. You watch it over and over again, and you laugh harder every time. The contest judges must think it's funny, too, because your movie is accepted into the film festival. Yay!

On opening night of the festival, you sit by Riley and Becca, whose "Winning Moments" movie was accepted, too. Only, your movie wins a first-place award, and theirs doesn't place at all.

"Great work," says Riley. "You deserve it."

Becca is quiet, though. She confesses later that she wishes the two of you could have worked on the same movie instead of making two different movies that were so similar. When you think about it, you *did* kind of borrow her idea. Maybe next time, you'll find a way to stick with your friends and work together. That's the only thing that could make this "winning moment" even sweeter.

The End

At the next rehearsal, you're feeling more comfortable behind the camera. But when Isabel walks onstage with an adorable chocolate Lab pup, you wish you were onstage, too, with all the other actors.

"This is Chocolate Chip," Neely says, introducing the pup. "Otherwise known as Prince Charming."

The puppy is adorable! Kayla thinks so, too. She sits down and lets him give her happy kisses.

Devin stands back, arms crossed. She's the only girl onstage who doesn't seem to be "charmed" by the pup. *How can she resist those big brown eyes?* you wonder as you record a few scenes of Prince Charming's grand entrance.

As you replay the footage back in your room that night, you watch as Devin tries to "dance" with her Prince Charming, who only wants to run back to Kayla—his real true love. The more frustrated Devin gets, the more she takes it out on Kayla.

If only Devin could see what she looks like when she acts that way, you think to yourself. It's like a behind-the-scenes reality TV show.

That thought gives you an idea.

 If you decide to record your own reality show, turn to page 61.

 If you decide to show Devin what she looks like onstage, turn to page 55.

As your movie ends, a few of your friends come over to congratulate you and Logan. Out of the corner of your eye, you see Jamie nudge the girl in the seat next to her. "That was more like a mock-umentary," she says loudly. "You can't always believe what you see on-screen." Jamie gives you a quick sideways glance, her eyes dancing as if she's sitting on a big secret.

You find out later, through the friend of a friend, just what Jamie's secret is. It turns out that she did a little behind-the-scenes trickery: she swapped your bean plant every night with a bigger one to make it look as if your plant was growing super fast. You're *mortified*.

Your movie ends up winning third place in the film festival, but neither you nor Logan feels very good about it.

You're angry with Jamie, but a part of you wonders if you could have prevented all this by letting her help out with the project from the start. Working *with* Jamie might have been easier than working against her.

You and Logan decide to talk to the contest judges to sort things out. As you walk down the winding hall, you reach for Logan's hand, grateful that whatever happens, at least you're in this *together*.

The End

You don't give the permission form much more thought. You're too busy searching for funny video clips. You even create a few of your own. You borrow a video camera from the yearbook office and hide out around campus, searching for hilarious moments to round out your movie.

You catch Isabel dancing when she thinks nobody's looking, and Logan doing yoga outside the Real Spirit Center, which is a really funny clip. Logan sure isn't very flexible!

When you're done stringing the clips together into a movie and editing it down, you couldn't be happier with it. It's going to win the contest for sure!

The movie *does* get accepted into the film festival, and as you watch it with your friends, you keep an eye on their faces. Nearly every one of your friends appears somewhere in this video, although some of them seem to appreciate it more than others. Logan looks a little annoyed about the yoga thing, but you're pretty sure she'll get over it.

Turn to page 53.

Luckily, Riley is back on her feet by the next afternoon.

"Feeling better?" you ask when she pokes her head into your room.

"Much," says Riley. "Thanks for working on the movie project while I was sick."

At the mention of the movie, your face falls. Riley picks right up on that. "Becca told me what happened," she says. "And you know what? You made the right call. You were being a good teammate and friend. Loyal friends make sure their friends don't get hurt."

You instantly feel better. *Riley has a knack for making everything look brighter,* you think.

 Turn to page 54.

Loyal friends make sure their friends don't get hurt.

When your movie ends, everyone applauds, but it's not quite the standing ovation you'd imagined. There's no time to dwell on that, though. Becca and Riley's "Winning Moments" movie is up next!

The movie is full of interesting moments, both bad and good. There's Becca scoring a goal, and there's Shelby scoring hers—at the wrong end of the field. You're about to search for her in the audience when you catch sight of the next face on-screen. It's *you*, tripping over your own feet as you dribble down the field. It's a little embarrassing, but you laugh anyway.

Then there's Riley, making a great save as goalie. And next up? You again—trying to make a similar save, but missing by a mile and landing on your face.

As you watch the movie, you can't help noticing that there seem to be more blooper clips of *you* than anyone else. What's up with that?

 Turn to page 82.

Now that Riley's better, you struggle to decide what to do about the movie project. You're pretty sure Becca is mad at you, after you shot down her "embarrassing moments" movie. You're not sure you want to keep working with her—or if *she'll* want to keep working with you.

You've also been wondering about Shelby. After you ran into her in the yearbook office, you got to thinking about how talented she is when it comes to photography. Maybe she has some *moviemaking* skills, too.

If you stick with the soccer movie, turn to page 64.

If you ask Shelby if she wants to work on a movie with you, turn to page 60.

You save the Devin scenes to a DVD. Then you write a note that says "Devin, I was deleting some extra footage and came across these scenes. I thought you might like to have them." You sign your name and drop the DVD in the campus mail, knowing it will reach Devin by tomorrow.

The next night at rehearsal, Devin shows up a little late. Instead of blaming someone or something, though, she apologizes and changes quickly into costume.

As Devin passes you, she says hello, but she doesn't quite look you in the eye. Is she embarrassed about the video? Maybe. But at least she's being nicer. She doesn't say anything when Kayla fumbles her lines in the first scene, and she even gives Chocolate Chip a kiss on the nose.

No one else will ever see the footage you shot of Devin, but your "movie" seems to have already made a difference. You're proud of yourself for sharing it with Devin in a respectful way—and for giving her a chance to change.

★The End ★

Logan seems disappointed when you tell her that you and Jamie are switching projects, but she shrugs and says, "That's okay. There's not a lot to do until we start editing the movie."

You promise Logan that you'll check in with her next week and see if she needs help editing her documentary. Then you hurry off to Pet-Palooza to find Amber.

You and Jamie help Amber with her last three days of recording. On the first day, you hold a treat in the air so that Amber can record Sugar, a little Yorkie pup, dancing in a circle. On the second day, you and Jamie take turns throwing a Frisbee to Pepper, a young husky, while Amber "catches" it all on video.

On the third day, you show up just in time to see something *really* special: Honey, a young golden retriever, is napping in a corner of the indoor play area, and curled up right beside her is Ginger, a little calico kitten.

 Turn to page 59.

The next night at rehearsal, you're thrilled to see that "Prince Charming" has arrived. You think the chocolate Lab is adorable, and he seems pretty fond of you, too. You drop down on your knees and give him a good belly rub.

"This is Chocolate Chip," Neely says, introducing the pup. "Otherwise known as Prince Charming."

Isabel fastens a tuxedo collar around Chocolate Chip's neck, and *presto,* he does look like a prince! Then she hands him a high-heeled shoe. "We're trying to get him to bring it to Devin in his mouth," she says, "but it's not working."

Devin calls Chocolate Chip by patting the side of her leg, but every time she does it, he runs the other way—usually to you. He's so cute that you can't help giving him kisses before sending him back toward Devin.

"Stop encouraging him," Devin snaps at you.

Wow. Not even an adorable dog can sweeten up Devin-ella. It's no wonder Chocolate Chip doesn't want to be around her, and you really don't either. You get up and head backstage, hoping the puppy doesn't follow you.

 Turn to page 74.

Ginger wakes up, yawns, and then starts grooming herself. Every once in a while, she licks Honey's paw, too.

"I didn't know cats and dogs could be friends," you say.

"They're *great* friends," says Amber. And they sure do seem to be.

Amber catches some of the cuddling on video. Then she brings another kitten into the play area, which perks Ginger right up. As Ginger gets up, stretches, and wanders over to sniff the other kitten, Honey lifts her head and whines a little.

"Aw," you say, "she doesn't want Ginger to go."

"I know," says Amber. "Honey is a pretty loyal pal."

While Ginger plays with the other kitten, Honey puts her head on her paws and stares at Ginger with sad puppy-dog eyes. The expression on her face is so sweet that it nearly breaks your heart. You sit beside Honey and give her some extra love before leaving Pet-Palooza for the day.

 Turn to page 62.

Riley is a little disappointed that you don't want to work on the soccer video anymore, but when you tell her you'd like to invite Shelby to do something, she understands.

"I don't think Shelby is working on a movie yet," Riley says. "You should definitely ask her. She'd be great at it!"

You knock on the door to Shelby's dorm room, but she's not there. As you're leaving Brightstar House to go in search of her, you see her walking just a little ways ahead of you down the path, a video camera hanging off her shoulder.

"Shelby, wait up!" you call to her.

She turns around and flashes a friendly smile, as always. "Hey," she says. "What're you up to?"

"Looking for you, actually," you say. "I was wondering if you wanted to work on a movie project with me."

Shelby shakes her curly head. "Sorry," she says. "I'd love to, but there's no time. I have to get this camera to Neely right away, and I promised Amber I'd show her how to do voice-overs for her movie. She's got some great footage of puppies," Shelby adds with a smile.

That Shelby. She's such a dependable friend—to everyone—but you know that must take a lot of time and energy.

 Turn to page 67.

You can picture the movie in your head. It'll be called *The REAL Cinderella.* Instead of featuring a sweet, friendly heroine, it'll feature "Devin-ella" at her worst—making fun of her stepsisters, fighting with her fairy godmother over her gown, and turning up her nose at Prince Charming, who doesn't want anything to do with her anyway.

You start editing your video right away, and as the next few days of rehearsal roll on, you add to your footage. Devin just keeps giving you better and better material to work with. Sometimes, you bring your camera with you backstage, because there are some interesting things happening there, too.

One day, you catch Megan tinkering with Cinderella's "glass" slipper in the wardrobe area. It looks as if she's stuffing tissue paper into the toe of the shoe. Your video camera is at your side, and you reach down as quietly as you can to push the record button.

Megan whirls around as you step closer. "Oh, it's you," she says, breathing a sigh of relief. She glances down at the wad of tissue paper in her hand. "It's just a joke," she says quickly, "to make sure that the glass slipper *doesn't* fit. Devin kind of deserves it, don't you think?"

You nod. You do think Devin deserves to be brought down a notch, and besides, this'll make a great scene in your movie.

 Turn to page 65.

You, Jamie, and Amber have fun together editing the video footage. Shelby helps, too, by showing you how to do *voice-overs*, or how to record yourselves talking at certain points in the movie to make it look as if the animals are saying the words. It's so cute!

You know the movie will be a big hit, so you're not surprised when it's accepted into the film festival. You go to the festival with Amber and Jamie.

Logan is there, too. *Uh-oh.* You suddenly remember that you never checked in with her to see if she needed help editing her documentary. You scan the list of films on your brochure and see that Logan's bean-growing movie didn't make the list. She looks a little sad. You get up to go talk to her, but just then, the lights go down.

"This is our movie!" Jamie whispers, pulling you back into your seat.

As you watch the film, you can't believe how well it turned out. There's Sugar, dancing in a little circle. You and Amber added music to the scene, and no one can see you in the shot, holding the treat above Sugar's head. It looks as if she's just enjoying the music, lost in her own little world.

Then there's Pepper, racing for the Frisbee, with Jamie's voice-over saying, "I got it! I got it! I've almost got it! Oops, I missed it. Throw it again. Throw it again! Please?" Every-one in the audience laughs, because if Pepper could talk, that's *just* what he would say.

 Turn to page 66.

You decide to stick with the soccer movie. You promised Riley you'd help her out, and you don't want to abandon her now—especially after she was so nice to you about the Becca thing.

You and Riley get back to work, combing the videos for some winning moments. As it turns out, there are plenty of them to choose from. Becca gets back on board with the project, too, when she sees just how many of those winning moments feature her.

When the movie is finished, you know it will be one you can be proud of. You're proud of yourself for being a loyal friend, too. Shelby may never know that you stood up for her and made sure Becca didn't embarrass her with the movie clips, but that's okay. You know Shelby would do the same for you.

The End

"Are you getting some good stuff?" Neely asks you later, midway through rehearsal. She peeks at your viewfinder.

"I am!" you say, which is true. You're filming plenty of great scenes for Neely's movie, but you're getting some good extra scenes for your reality version, too.

For some reason, you don't tell Neely about your project just yet, but you decide to tell Kayla. Devin is being so mean to her during the final scenes of filming that you figure she could use a pick-me-up. You invite her to your room to watch the footage of Devin-ella.

Kayla's jaw drops when she sees how you strung together all of Devin's most "dramatic" moments.

"Wow," she says, giggling. "What are you going to do with all this?"

You tell Kayla your plans for entering your reality-show version of *Cinderella* in the contest, which you think she'll support. After all, this is *great* stuff—it's bound to win a place in the film festival!

Instead, though, Kayla is silent. Then she says, "Are you sure that's the right thing to do?"

 Turn to page 71.

The final scene shows Honey cuddling with Ginger. When Ginger gets up to go, Honey lifts her head, and you hear Amber's sweet voice-over saying "No, don't go! Wait, old buddy, old pal. Stay here with me!"

Then the film actually plays *backward*, with Ginger walking back to Honey, stretching, and nestling in beside her. The scene fades to black with the words "Loyal to the End" popping up in a big heart on-screen. That was your idea—a nice finishing touch.

The audience starts clapping, which makes you feel good, but then you catch sight of Logan sliding out of her seat and heading down the aisle toward the door. Suddenly, your guilt is back. Sure, you made a great film with Amber. But you also abandoned Logan in the process. If you had stayed with her, loyal to the end, would she have finished her movie and had it featured in the film festival, too? You'll never know.

You slide out of your seat and head after Logan. It's time to find out how your friend's doing—and whether there's anything you can do for her now.

The End

"No worries," you say to Shelby. "It sounds like you have your hands full."

Shelby frowns and nods, but then she perks back up. "It's fun stuff," she says. "I can't complain!" And then she's off down the trail again, heading toward U-Shine Hall.

As you watch Shelby walk, you wish there was something you could do to show her how much you and your friends appreciate her.

Then it hits you: maybe you can use the movie contest as a way to pay tribute to Shelby, "Photographer and Friend Extraordinaire."

You're not a filmmaker, though, and if you want to keep this a surprise, you can't ask Shelby for help. Who else might be able to help you?

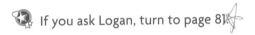 If you ask Logan, turn to page 81.

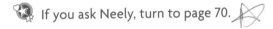 If you ask Neely, turn to page 70.

 If you ask Amber, turn to page 72.

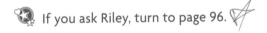 If you ask Riley, turn to page 96.

Logan is so desperate to find an answer that you have to look at all the possibilities, even if it means making a fool of yourself. You giggle nervously as you tell Logan about Neely's grandma's advice.

Logan doesn't laugh, though—she takes you seriously. You should have known she would.

She pulls out a pen and a little notebook from her backpack. "So, how long did you sing?" she asks, her pen poised to take notes. "And how close were you to the plant?"

"Um . . . I'm not sure," you say. "Maybe for a few minutes? And I was probably about a foot away."

"Like this?" asks Logan, setting down her notebook and leaning over the plant.

"Yeah," you say. "Something like that."

"Got it," she says. "I'll start doing it, too. Let's shoot for six minutes at a time, or even twelve. And keep track of how long you sing, okay?" Logan taps her notebook, always the scientist.

Twelve minutes? You wish you knew a few more lullabies.

 Turn to page 89.

You know that Neely is directing and filming her own Cinderella movie, so she must have a lot of moviemaking experience. Maybe she can help you create something for Shelby.

"Actually, Shelby's the one who showed me how to use the video recorder," says Neely, when you find her just outside of U-Shine Hall. "I'd never really used one until she taught me."

"Really?" you say, thinking how brave Neely is to take on a full production as her first project.

"*Really,*" says Neely, as if she can't believe it herself. "So I owe Shelby a big thanks. We should definitely do something nice for her. But what?"

Turn to page 104.

Kayla's question surprises you. You don't know what to say.

"Devin has been awful," she says, "but if you enter that movie in the film contest, how will that make Neely feel? She might think you went behind her back to do this."

"But it's a totally different movie," you protest, even though a part of you knows Kayla is right. If you really think Neely will be okay with your movie, why haven't you told her about it yet?

You decide to sit on your video footage for a while until you can figure out what to do with it. But after Kayla leaves, you get an e-mail from Megan.

"Hey," she writes. "Kayla told me you had some pretty interesting video of Devin-ella. I'd love to see it. She's driving me crazy!"

If you bring a copy of the video to rehearsal, turn to page 77.

If you choose a scene or two to e-mail to Megan, turn to page 114.

If you decide not to share the video with Megan, turn to page 73.

You remember Shelby saying that she was going to help Amber with some voice-overs. Amber will probably be looking for a way to thank Shelby, too. Maybe the two of you can work together.

You know Shelby is hanging out with Amber this afternoon, so you wait until the next day to talk with Amber. You see her in line at the cafeteria, and you quickly step in behind her.

"Hey, Amber," you whisper. "I have a favor to ask you." You explain to Amber what you're hoping to do—find a way to thank Shelby for everything she does for her friends at Innerstar U—and Amber jumps right on board.

"Shelby has been great," she says. "You should hear the voice-overs she helped me record for my movie. They're so cute!"

Talking about voice-overs leads to a great idea. You can hardly wait to get started!

 Turn to page 76.

Even though you shared the video with Kayla, you don't feel quite right about sharing it with Megan. Maybe it's because she has her own role in the footage, messing with Cinderella's glass slipper backstage. Or maybe it's because Kayla's words got you thinking about whether making the movie is the right thing to do.

Either way, you e-mail Megan to tell her that the video isn't ready to share. Then you watch the video again, trying to figure out what to do with it.

By the time the video ends, you still don't have a plan, but you know who might be able to help you: Neely. You feel bad about not having told her about the video before. Maybe if you finally 'fess up, she can help you decide what to do next.

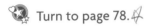 Turn to page 78.

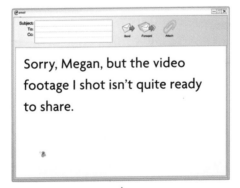

You watch from backstage as Neely comes up with an ingenious way to get Chocolate Chip to go to Devin. Neely brought a BLT sandwich—her dinner—to rehearsal. She pulls a slice of bacon out of the sandwich.

"Here," she says to Devin, "try this."

Devin scrunches up her face. "Ew," she says. "That's gross."

"Maybe," says Neely, "but it could work!"

It *does* work. Chocolate Chip learns that every time he goes to Devin, he gets a bite of bacon. Pretty soon, he runs onstage with the shoe in his mouth and scampers directly to her, dropping the shoe and plastering her hand with kisses until she gives him the bacon.

Devin must be the only girl you know who doesn't like puppy kisses. "Ew, get off me," she says to Chocolate Chip when the scene ends. The pup whines and sits, trying to please her, but when he doesn't get the petting he hopes for, he wanders backstage and finds you.

You're giving Chocolate Chip a good scratch behind the ears when Megan sits down beside you. "Are you okay?" she asks. "Devin can be kind of tough to take."

You sigh. "Yeah," you say. "I'm sure I'll get used to it."

"You shouldn't have to," says Megan. "She's being mean. I think it's time to give her a taste of her own medicine."

If you agree with Megan, turn to page 84.

If you disagree with her, turn to page 87.

You head to Amber's room the next afternoon. She shows you the footage she has of some of the pets at Pet-Palooza. Your favorite scene is of Ginger, a calico kitten, curled up beside a golden retriever, Honey. That's the scene Amber thinks will work best for your thank-you to Shelby.

By the time the two of you are done, the scene is even more precious than it was to begin with. You watch the finished video on-screen.

There's Honey, waking up from her nap and opening her mouth in a lazy yawn. Then Honey starts "talking," courtesy of Amber's voice. She says, "Thanks for watching our movie. I hope you enjoyed it as much as I enjoyed that nap. And thanks to Shelby for teaching us how to speak."

At that moment, Honey licks Ginger's head, and you hear Honey saying, "It's your turn, Ginger. Speak!"

Ginger opens her mouth to let out what's probably a little meow, but with your voice-over, Ginger says in a squeaky voice, "Thanks to Shelby, a loyal friend to the end."

The picture slowly fades away until there's nothing left but the words "The End" in a little red heart. Shelby will *love* this. And who knows? Maybe when the excitement of the film festival dies down, you and Shelby can use some of what you've learned today to make a *new* movie together—one that's all about friendship.

 The End

You bring a copy of the video to rehearsal the next day, and Megan slips it into her backpack. "Thanks," she says. "I can hardly wait to watch this!"

Kayla sees you give the DVD to Megan, and she looks worried. It turns out that *you* should be, too. That night, you get a nasty e-mail from Megan. She writes, "I can't believe you recorded me backstage messing with that shoe. How would you feel if I'd done that to you?"

Uh-oh. The shoe incident. You'd forgotten about that.

You write back a quick apology, but Megan isn't satisfied. "I want you to delete that right away," she says. "If Neely sees it, I'll be in big trouble."

You tell Megan that you'll delete the scene, but you don't really want to. Your visions of an award-winning video are slowly slipping away.

If you leave your video as is, turn to page 79.

If you delete the shoe scene, turn to page 85.

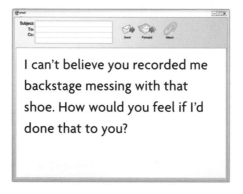

I can't believe you recorded me backstage messing with that shoe. How would you feel if I'd done that to you?

When you invite Neely over and show her the Devin scenes you recorded, she's confused. "What are these?" she asks. "Are they outtakes?"

Outtakes are bloopers or mistakes that a filmmaker cuts out of a movie while editing it. You never thought of the Devin scenes as outtakes, but you guess they kind of are.

"What a great idea!" Neely says. "Maybe we could run them at the end of the movie, as a bonus. I mean, we'd have to get permission from the actors first—especially Devin. There sure are a lot of her in here."

You clear your throat. "Yeah," you say, "there sure are." What you're thinking is, *There's no way Devin is going to give you permission to show those.* But you're wrong.

Devin doesn't want *all* the outtakes of her to be shown, but she agrees to a few of them, like the scene where Prince Charming knocks her down onstage and gives her a few slobbery kisses. She even giggles a bit at that one.

Seeing Devin laugh at herself makes you think that maybe she's not all that bad. Or maybe your filmmaking is helping her see herself in a different way. Either way, you're glad you were honest with Neely about the video. She'll help you bring your filmmaking to the big screen—and make sure that no one gets hurt along the way.

 The End

As the deadline for entering the movie contest approaches, you struggle to figure out what to do. You think you have a pretty good chance of winning a spot in the film festival with this movie. You'd like to give it your best shot, and that means leaving it as is—shoe scene and all.

You decide to enter the movie in the contest just to see how it does. You can always pull it later if you need to, right?

After dropping off a DVD of your movie with the judges at U-Shine Hall, you watch your e-mail for three days straight. On the third day, you get the word: your movie didn't make the final cut. You wonder why, but you don't have to wonder for long. You hear a loud knock on your door. It's Devin, and she's *really* mad.

"I can't believe you betrayed me that way," Devin says, tears threatening her eyes. It turns out that a friend of Devin's was one of the students on the judging panel. She saw the movie and told Devin all about it.

Worse yet, Devin tells Neely about your movie. Neely is really hurt that you went behind her back and made your own version of *Cinderella*. You try to explain, but what can you say? You entered the movie in the festival even though two people—and your conscience—told you not to. You didn't win a place in the festival. Instead, you might have just lost a friend.

 The End

By Monday, it seems as if your Devin-ella video clips have traveled all across campus. You can't leave your room without someone mentioning them, and you're guessing that Devin can't either. She doesn't show up at rehearsal Monday night. You're kind of afraid to go, too, because you're pretty sure Neely will be upset with you.

As it turns out, Neely isn't upset. Maybe she's the only girl on campus who has been too busy to check her e-mail lately. Or maybe she doesn't have time to be upset with you because she's too worried about the fact that Devin, her star actor, has gone missing.

Either way, you know what you have to do: apologize to Devin and then get rid of the rest of that video footage. You can't take back the video clips that are already out there in cyberspace, but you can make sure that no more clips get posted online. You owe Devin that much.

The End

Logan knows Shelby well, and she's great at figuring out how things work. If you need some tips on photography or on combining photos to make a video for Shelby, Logan's your gal.

You know Logan is working on a bean-plant movie, so you search for her at the Blue Sky Nature Center. There she is—kneeling in front of a small pot of black soil. "Staring at it won't make it grow," you tease as you step up behind her.

Logan blushes as she turns around. "Are you sure?" she asks. "Is that a scientific fact?"

You shrug. "I don't know," you say, laughing. "That's your department."

When you tell Logan what you're up to, she's excited to help out. "Shelby spent a lot of time showing me how to set up this tripod," she says. "I'd like to thank her, too."

"Good," you say. "Maybe we can do something together. Do you have any ideas?"

Turn to page 86.

By the end of the movie, you're not laughing anymore. You definitely had the starring role in the movie, and everyone in the audience seems to think it's a whole lot funnier than you do.

Becca jokes with you after the film festival. "That's what you get," she says, "for abandoning our 'winning moments' video and going out on a mission to embarrass every girl on campus." She punches your arm playfully, but it kind of hurts.

Actually, what hurts is your pride. You force a smile. What else can you do? Becca's right—you sort of deserve what you got. Maybe next time, you'll take Shelby's advice and get permission before doing anything that could embarrass your friends. It could save *you* a big dose of embarrassment, too.

 **The End**

You can't help agreeing with Megan. You don't like the way Devin is treating people, and her attitude is making Neely's job as director tougher, too.

"What should we do?" you ask Megan.

She grins mischievously, a glint in her brown eyes. "Well, for starters," she says, "we can make sure that the glass slipper *doesn't* fit Cinderella."

You stifle a giggle. You like the way Megan thinks.

During a break before the next scene, you help Megan sneak the slipper offstage and bring it to the wardrobe area. Megan stuffs some tissue into the toe of the slipper and then hands it back to you. "That ought to do it," she whispers, giving you a silent high five.

 Turn to page 88.

You hate to lose the shoe scene, but you have to respect Megan's wishes. In fact, her reaction gets you thinking about how *you'd* feel if someone recorded you without asking—and then threatened to put the scene in a movie that the entire campus would see.

You delete the shoe scene and rewatch the video. You still have great footage, but you're less excited about it now. You've been so carried away with the idea of revealing the "truth" about Devin, but the truth is, you've kind of known all along that this movie was a bad idea.

What's a better idea? Getting rid of all the behind-the-scenes footage and finding some *real* scenes to give to Neely. Her movie is the one that should be in the film festival, and to get it there, she's going to need your help.

 **The End**

Logan suggests adding a thank-you to Shelby in the last scene of her bean-plant movie. "Just as the plant reaches its full height," Logan says, spreading her arms in the air dramatically, "words could flash across the screen that say 'special thanks to our good friend Shelby, whose ideas and support helped this movie *grow.*'"

"That's good," you say, nodding encouragingly. "And maybe we can even put a picture of Shelby's face on one of the top leaves of the plant?"

"Hmm . . ." says Logan. "Kind of corny, but cute!"

You're excited about both ideas, and you think Shelby will be, too. When Logan asks if you want to play on her computer for a while, figuring out how to use movie-making software to add photographs and words to videos, you say yes.

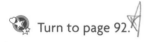 Turn to page 92.

You're tempted to join forces with Megan, but you don't want to sink to Devin's level.

"Fighting back isn't going to help," you say to Megan. "That'll just make Devin more mad—and more mean."

Megan sighs. "You're probably right," she says. "So, what do we do?"

You think of Neely, who is working hard to keep the production on track. "I guess we just do our best with the parts we have and try not to let Devin get to us."

Megan doesn't look so sure about your plan, but she finally shrugs and says hesitantly, "Okay. I'll give it my best shot."

Turn to page 90.

It's hard to watch the next scene without bursting out laughing. Devin tries to slip her foot into the shoe while Prince Charming, sitting obediently, looks on. But the shoe just doesn't fit. Devin stands up and starts stomping her foot onto the stage in a very non-princess-like way. The noise scares Chocolate Chip, who runs away with his tail between his legs.

"Cut!" calls Neely as Isabel steps onstage to try to help Devin.

"I thought you measured my foot!" says Devin. "You must have messed up."

"I don't know," jokes Isabel. "Have your feet grown?"

The joke falls flat. Devin isn't in the mood for humor, and Neely isn't either. "We're running out of time," she says with an exasperated sigh. "We have a lot to get through tonight."

You check your watch. It *is* getting late, but you have to admit that seeing Devin squirm onstage felt pretty good. When Megan pulls you aside to tell you about her next plan, you're all ears.

 Turn to page 112.

After dinner that night, you stop at the library to search for song lyrics on the Internet. You need new material. But printing off lyrics takes longer than you thought it would. By the time you leave, it's dark outside. The nature center will be closing in fifteen minutes!

You sprint through the plaza. When you get to the nature center, it's empty—except for the volunteer at the front desk. She looks annoyed that you're coming so late, so you promise her that you'll only stay a minute.

You tiptoe quietly through the greenhouse, as if the plants around you are babies sleeping in a nursery. You round the corner of a long aisle of plants and turn toward the shelf where your bean plant is perched. Someone's there beside it. Logan?

No, it's someone else—*Jamie*. She has your bean plant in one hand and is holding another plant in her other hand. What's she doing?

"Jamie!" you say, louder than you meant to. She jumps and drops a pot, which lands with a *crack* on the ground.

Turn to page 93.

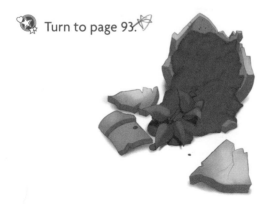

Not letting Devin get to you turns out to be easier said than done. At the next rehearsal, you're reshooting an early scene that Kayla is having trouble with. She has several lines in a row, and she keeps messing them up. It doesn't help that Devin is getting frustrated with her.

Kayla tries one of her lines again: "I just heard that the king is throwing a ball to find his wife, Prince Charming, a son."

Devin snorts. "Want to try that again?" she says sharply. "The line is 'I just heard that the king is throwing a ball to find his *son*, Prince Charming, a *wife*."

Kayla clamps her mouth shut. She looks as if she's never going to open it again, at least not while Devin is onstage.

You want to snap back at Devin. You're fed up with her attitude. It's one thing for her to treat you badly. It's another thing for her to come down on Kayla, who is trying her hardest. But if you say something, you'll just make things harder for Neely, who is having enough trouble getting this scene shot.

 If you speak up and say something to Devin, turn to page 94.

 If you stay quiet, turn to page 118.

If you say something to Kayla, go online to innerstarU.com/secret and enter this code: URLOYAL

Logan's bean-plant documentary makes it into the film festival, and Shelby is right there in the audience when the movie starts to roll. You can't wait for the end, when Shelby's name and face will flash on-screen.

When they finally appear, Shelby squeals. "Oh!" she says. "I can't believe you guys did that!" You can tell that the credit made her feel pretty good.

You notice that *lots* of girls thank Shelby for her help after the film festival ends. She may not have made her own movie, but she was right there helping out her friends behind the scenes.

You feel as if you did a pretty good job, too, of being a "behind the scenes" friend to Shelby today. And you helped Logan make a better movie along the way!

The End

"What are you doing?" you ask Jamie as you walk toward her, stepping around a shard of pot on the ground.

Jamie laughs and raises her hands. "Alright, you caught me," she says. "I was just having a little fun with your magic bean."

You look down at your poor bean plant, lying on the ground with its roots exposed. "What did you *do*?" you groan, sinking to the floor and reaching for the plant.

"Oh, settle down," says Jamie. "That's not yours. I swapped out your puny plant two days ago."

When Jamie sees the look of confusion on your face, she lets out an exaggerated sigh. Then she tells you that she's been sneaking in at night and swapping plants to make it look as if yours is growing super fast. She sounds almost proud of the way she sabotaged the project.

You're speechless. You're so mad at Jamie that you can barely breathe.

As always, Jamie can't understand why you're upset. "I was just having some fun," she says. "And think of how cool this'll look in your movie. Having a super-fast-growing plant makes it better," she says. "It's like special effects."

You shake your head at Jamie and storm out of the greenhouse. You've got to find Logan right away.

 Turn to page 95.

You can't stand it—you have to say something. "Back off, Devin," you say loudly. "Kayla's doing her best."

There's sudden silence on the set. Everyone turns to look at you. Even Kayla looks shocked that you said something.

Devin narrows her eyes. She's about to fire back at you, but Neely steps onstage with her hands in a T-shape. "Time-out," she says. "Let's take a break."

You feel as if you just made Neely's job harder, not easier. As she walks your way, you mouth the word *sorry*.

Neely shakes her head and then says quietly, "It's okay. Someone had to say something to Devin. You were right to stand strong for Kayla. That's what friends do."

 Turn to page 98.

Loyal friends stand strong for each other.

Logan isn't in her room or at the library, one of her favorite hangouts. You've run out of obvious places to look, so you go to bed. You'll have to try again tomorrow.

The next morning, before you can find Logan, she finds you—just leaving your room for breakfast.

"You *have* to come to my room," Logan says. "I swapped memory cards on the camera in the greenhouse and brought home the photos we've shot so far. I downloaded the shots onto my computer and strung them together into a video, and it's *so* cool!"

You open your mouth to tell Logan about Jamie's prank, but something prevents you from speaking. Maybe it's the excitement in Logan's green eyes. You follow her to her room, waiting for the right moment to tell her the truth.

As you watch Logan's video, though, you have to admit it *is* super cool. As each day turns into night, the picture dims, and then the plant springs up the next morning larger and more full of life than the night before. You try to catch evidence of Jamie's mischief in the video, but there's nothing. The pots are the same, and the plants are similar enough to seem like the same plant—only bigger. If you weren't so mad at Jamie, you'd be sort of impressed.

Now you have a choice to make.

If you tell Logan about Jamie's prank, turn to page 100.

If you stay quiet, turn to page 110.

You feel a little funny going back to Riley and asking for her help with Shelby's video. But Riley is such a team player, and she's the one who said that you should do something with Shelby. Maybe Riley will have some ideas about what you can do *for* Shelby.

You find Riley in the yearbook office looking for more soccer clips. When you ask for her help, her face lights up. "I have something we can use," she says. "I just came across this footage of Shelby scoring her first goal. Check it out!"

The video is perfect. Shelby looks *so* excited after the goal. You remember how hard she worked during that game and how proud she seemed when your teammates lifted her onto their shoulders to celebrate.

"What should we do with it?" Riley asks.

"Well, it's definitely a 'winning moment,'" you say. "Maybe it deserves a special place in your movie."

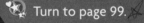 Turn to page 99.

"Devin is being *awful*," Neely continues, "but we just don't have time to find a new Cinderella. I'm afraid we're stuck with her."

Neely looks at you with such miserable eyes that you get angry at Devin all over again. You rack your brain trying to think of someone else who could play the lead role. You suddenly remember the conversation you overheard between Megan and Devin on your first day on the set.

"What about Megan?" you think out loud. "Didn't she try out for the role of Cinderella, too?"

Neely glances back at the actors milling around backstage. "Megan," she says thoughtfully. "Yeah, I think she did. Actually, she was pretty good—not as dramatic as Devin, but maybe that's a good thing." She smiles at you sheepishly. "But wait—if Megan plays Cinderella, who's going to be the evil stepmother?"

Good question, you think to yourself, but you reassure Neely that you'll figure it out. "I'll help you find someone," you promise her.

Neely looks relieved for the first time in days. "Thanks," she says. "Now I just have to break the news to Devin. Wish me luck."

 Turn to page 101.

The clip of Shelby's goal gets the *most* special place in the movie: the closing scene. You're sitting beside Shelby during the film festival when the movie plays, and when she catches sight of herself on-screen, she covers her mouth with her hands, her eyes bright. It's like she's replaying that moment over again. You know *just* how she feels.

"It's kind of a rush, isn't it?" you whisper to her as the screen fades to black.

Shelby nods. "I haven't felt like that in a long time," she whispers back. "At least, not till right now."

Shelby squeezes your hand, which makes you feel pretty good, too. You didn't enter a movie in the contest, but you created something even more special: another winning moment for Shelby, who deserved one most of all.

☆The End☆

The video is definitely cool, but you just can't keep the truth from Logan. You turn your back to the computer screen and lean against the edge of her desk.

"Logan, here's the thing," you say, your voice a little wobbly. "It isn't real. Jamie pulled another one of her stupid pranks."

Logan's smile slowly fades. "What?" she asks hoarsely, her eyes narrowing. "What'd she do?"

You explain it all to Logan, who sinks lower and lower in her chair as she listens. When you finish, she stares at the floor, unblinking.

"Now what?" she asks in a small voice. "We can't start over. We won't have time to edit our video if we have to grow a whole new plant, especially a normal slow-growing plant." Logan groans. "I guess we just have to skip this year's contest," she says.

 If you feel like quitting, too, turn to page 102.

 If you stay with Logan till you figure out another idea, turn to page 108.

Neely talks with Devin right away after rehearsal. She tells you the next day that it was the hardest conversation she's ever had with Devin, but that it helped to know that you were backing up her decision.

Megan is thrilled to step into the role of Cinderella. As soon as she agrees to the part, you and the rest of the actors put your heads together to come up with a replacement for her role as evil stepmother.

"How about Emmy?" suggests Kayla. "She told me the other day that she wishes she'd tried out for a part."

"Yes!" you say. Emmy is a good friend of yours at Innerstar U.

You offer to ask Emmy about the part that night at dinner, and when you do, she says *yes*. You stay late a few nights after rehearsal to help her learn her lines quickly.

 Turn to page 103.

You nod sadly. "Yeah," you say. "I guess there's always next year."

You sit for a while, trying to think of something comforting to say to Logan, but you've got nothing. You give her shoulder a squeeze and then leave here there, slumped over in her desk chair. You're pretty sure she just wants to be alone right now, and you sort of do, too.

You know you did the right thing by telling Logan the truth, but you wish there was more you could do for her. As you walk out her door, you realize that there *is*. You can stick with her—and with the movie—and figure out a new plan. You decide to go back to your room and pull out a little notebook of your own, which you'll fill with helpful ideas for your friend.

The End

After filming the last scene, Isabel, Neely, Megan, and Kayla present you with a small gift. You can tell through the wrapping paper what it is: the fairy godmother's wand.

"Because you helped save the show," Neely says. "Thanks for being a great stepsister."

"And stepdaughter," Megan jokes.

"And a loyal friend," adds Kayla sincerely. She's grateful that you stood up for her, and for *that*, you may be proudest of all.

The End

Before you and Neely can figure out a plan, you're interrupted by a furry flurry of excitement. Amber is walking a young brown Labrador, and he wants to stop and say hello to you and Neely. He jumps up on Neely's legs.

"*Down*, Chocolate Chip!" Amber scolds the hyper pup, giving his leash a gentle tug. "Where are your manners?"

Petting Chocolate Chip distracts you and Neely from your brainstorming, but he's actually the one who helps you come up with a way to thank Shelby.

Neely explains that Chocolate Chip is playing a role in *Cinderella*. "He's Prince Charming," she says, giggling. "Picture him in that closing scene when he and Cinderella dance off into the moonlight."

At the word *dance*, Chocolate Chip stands up on his back legs. "See?" says Amber proudly. "There's a well-trained boy!"

 Turn to page 107.

Making this new version of the video is fun. Paige helps you and Logan find other plants to feature in your video. Your tiny bean plant turns into a dandelion, which turns into a daisy, and—in the final scene—turns into a giant sunflower. That one wows you every time you see it.

By the time you enter the movie in the contest, you're feeling really good about it, and Logan is, too. You didn't help her grow a magic bean plant, but you did stay by her side and help her come up with a creative way to save the video. You feel like a real moviemaker now—and a loyal friend.

★ The End ★

After talking with Neely about how her movie will end, the two of you come up with a plan. You don't tell anyone—least of all Shelby—because you want it to be a big surprise at the film festival.

On opening night, you sit next to Neely and Shelby, listening to her giggle as she watches Prince Charming and Cinderella "dance" across the screen. The picture fades out, and then there he is: Chocolate Chip, still dressed in his royal costume, holding a sign in his mouth. It reads, "And they lived happily ever after, thanks to help from Shelby, Fairy Godmother and Filmmaker."

Chocolate Chip drops the sign and barks once just as Shelby squeals. "Oh!" she says. "That's so cute! Thank you!"

Loyal, dependable Shelby *is* kind of like a fairy god-mother, because she always magically appears just when you need her most. Tonight, she needed a little recognition, and you feel good about waving your *own* magic wand and making sure she got it.

 The End

You sit quietly beside Logan for a while. You think about the video—how Jamie swapped plants at night so the differences between the plants were blurred in the darkness. Suddenly, an idea strikes.

"Logan!" you say. "What if we keep making this video, swapping out bigger and bigger plants each night?"

Logan shakes her head. "That's not honest,"

she says. "I don't want to make a *fake* documentary."

"Who says we have to make a documentary?" you ask. "What if we get creative? I mean, we don't have to stick with bean plants. Maybe our bean grows up to be a daisy. Or better yet, a sunflower. Or . . ."

Logan's eyes light up. She pulls out her notebook and starts sketching ideas.

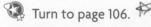 Turn to page 106.

You don't want to be the one to burst Logan's bubble. You convince yourself that no harm will come from sitting on the truth. But you're wrong.

Logan is so excited about documenting the growth of the "magic bean plant" that she has to show the video to Paige right away. She calls Paige and invites her to her room. When Paige shows up, Logan runs the movie again while you hold your breath—and your tongue—wondering what to do.

Unfortunately, Paige immediately suspects that something's up. "That's a really cool video," she says, "but beans don't grow that quickly. It's just not possible."

"Oh, but it is!" says Logan. "We discovered a way to speed up the growth: singing. Well, I think it's more about direct delivery of carbon dioxide to the plant . . ." she explains scientifically, "but we recorded all of that. Do you want to see my notes?"

Paige shakes her head. "No," she says, "but I want to see this plant."

The three of you head off to the greenhouse to check out the plant, which is every bit as leafy and green as the video showed. Paige picks up the pot and inspects it.

"This isn't the same plant," she announces. "The pot I gave you had a bigger drainage plate underneath it because I knew you'd be watering it a lot. I think someone must have accidentally switched plants."

Or not-so-accidentally, you think to yourself, trying to act as shocked as Logan looks right now.

Logan's face is bright red. "I—I don't get it," she stammers. "I thought we were really on to something."

Paige shrugs. "Sorry," she says. "You still have a pretty cool video, though."

Logan stares at the floor. "Yeah," she sighs, "except it's not real."

You feel a pang of guilt. Logan is all about the truth, about getting her facts straight. You thought you were protecting her by keeping Jamie's prank a secret, but you know now that you should have told Logan the truth instead of letting her embarrass herself in front of Paige.

"Come on," you say to Logan. "Maybe we can grow another bean. We'll figure something out."

You decide to get another bean and to tend to it yourself, this time in the safety of your own room. You'll help Logan start over, because that's what loyal friends do.

 **The End**

It's the final scene of the movie—the part where the fairy godmother waves her wand and changes Cinderella's rags back into a ballgown. Cinderella and her prince are supposed to dance together, just as they did at the ball.

You can tell by Devin's clenched hand that she has her bacon ready, and when Prince Charming is let off his leash, he heads straight for Devin. What Devin *doesn't* know is that you and Megan tucked tiny pieces of bacon into the pockets of her gown.

As Devin leans over to lift the pup's front paws into a dance, he noses at her pockets, searching for the hidden bacon. When he jumps up on her legs, Devin trips and falls backward, landing awkwardly in a pile of gold satin. Chocolate Chip leaps onto her chest and starts giving her face a good licking.

You're trying so hard not to snicker, but when your eyes meet Megan's, you can't hold it in anymore. You both burst out laughing—and you just can't stop.

Isabel rushes onstage to help Devin stand up, and when she does, you immediately spot the big rip in the hem of her gown. Isabel sees it, too. She sinks to her knees to inspect the fabric, her face nearly as pale as the gown.

That's when you see Neely's expression. She's standing there by the video camera, her hands hanging helplessly at her sides, and her face is all screwed up. She's not laughing. She's trying to keep from crying.

 Turn to page 115.

You eagerly choose a couple of funny scenes to send to Megan. Kayla may not have appreciated the video, but you're pretty sure Megan will—and you're right. She sends back a response right away. "LOL!" she writes. "Devin-ella strikes again. This is so funny!"

Megan's e-mail makes you feel pretty good. Maybe there's hope for your movie yet. You go to bed that night and dream of your dazzling future, walking the red carpet with other famous moviemakers and even a celebrity or two.

You wake up Saturday morning disappointed that you won't have rehearsal for the next two days. As you head toward the student center for breakfast, you remind your-self that you have plenty of work to do on the footage you've already shot. You need to edit your movie, and you have to make sure you have some good scenes to give Neely for her movie, too.

As you walk into the cafeteria, you bump into Becca, a girl you know from soccer. "Hey," you say absentmindedly, still planning out your day ahead.

"Hey!" says Becca brightly. Then she leans in and whispers, "I loved your video. Devin-ella. Ha!"

 Turn to page 116.

Guilt washes over you. You've been so focused on getting back at Devin that you forgot whom you were hurting in the process: Neely. Every time you "tripped up" Devin, you messed up Neely's production, too, and put her further and further behind.

Megan is nudging you in the arm now, giggling over the success of your "evil" plot twist, but you don't feel like celebrating. You step around her and hurry toward Neely, who's definitely crying now.

When you reach Neely, you put your hand on her shoulder. "It's okay," you say gently. "We'll get the show back on track. I promise."

As Neely wipes her face, you make a mental list of things you're going to do differently from now on. You're not going to sink to Devin's level anymore. You're going to focus on your *own* role in the play. And you're going to be a better friend to Neely—a friend she can depend on.

 **The End**

It takes a moment for Becca's words to register. *Devin-ella?* Megan must have shared your video clips with Becca.

Just then another girl in line congratulates you on the video. Now you're getting nervous. If these two girls saw the video, how many others did, too?

Megan answers that for you when you see her in the hallway at Brightstar House. "I sent it to a bunch of girls," she says, holding up her cell phone. "It was too good not to share."

You're shocked. It never occurred to you that Megan would share the video with other people without asking you. There's a sinking feeling in your chest, which gets worse when you run into Devin on campus later that day.

You can tell by the look on Devin's face that she knows about the video. She looks mad—an expression you know well—but she also seems really hurt.

Your reality show seems a lot less funny now that you see how hurtful it can be, even to someone as seemingly tough as Devin. The reality is that by sharing the video, you're no better than she is. At least when she hurts people, she does it to their face instead of behind their back.

As Devin turns around and quickly walks away, you know you should go after her—but what would you say?

 Turn to page 80.

You give Kayla a supportive smile, but you say nothing. And for the next week, you bite your tongue to stay quiet every time Devin picks on Kayla or does something that annoys you. *Just let it go,* you tell yourself, *for Neely's sake.*

Finally, all the scenes are shot, and Neely gets to work editing the footage to enter in the contest. You cross your fingers, hoping that the movie will make it into the festival, and it does!

The night of the festival, you sit in the audience at U-Shine Hall, watching the movie on-screen. It turned out really well—the costumes are beautiful, and Neely did a great job filming the movie. You even have to admit that Devin is a pretty good actress. She comes across as sweet and angelic as any Cinderella you've ever seen.

But every time you watch a scene with Kayla, you cringe, remembering how badly Devin treated her. You glance around the theater. Kayla isn't even here. You guess that by the time the movie was done filming, she'd had enough.

As the credits roll on the big screen, you see your name next to Kayla's, right after "ugly stepsisters." For a moment, you imagine different words: "loyal friend." Maybe that'll be your *next* starring role, if you get another chance.

The End